The Quiet Before Goodbye

A Story of Leaving Quietly and Loving Yourself Loudly

Julia West

Copyright

Table of Contents

Prologue

The Sound of Her Silence

They always talked about the moment a heart breaks like it would come with noise.

Shouting. Slamming doors. A scream into the dark. Glass crashing. A sob into the sink.

But hers didn't come with any of those.

When Olivia's heart broke, it didn't make a sound.
It simply stopped hoping.

It was quieter than breath. Quieter than memory.
And in that silence, finally, painfully, she heard herself.

Not the woman she had practiced being. Not the wife. Not the partner who had learned to shrink her voice to keep the peace.
She heard the version of herself who had been whispering beneath years of compromise.

The version who used to laugh too loudly.
The one who painted sunrises in wild colors and left her

coffee half-drunk because she was too busy dreaming.
The one who wanted more than a polished apartment and a man who touched her only out of habit.

That version had been waiting.
Beneath the forgiveness.
Beneath the small betrayals.
Beneath the lavender candles and late-night excuses.

And she had waited long enough.

It didn't start with the woman in the bed.

It started long before—in the way Ethan stopped looking at her with curiosity.
In the way he started answering her with half-smiles and distracted nods.
In the way her love letters turned into reminders about bills.
In the way he would forget her favorite wine but remember his assistant's coffee order.

She didn't walk out because he cheated.

She walked out because he had stopped choosing her long before he chose someone else.

They had built a life filled with routines.
Tuesday takeout.

Weekend Netflix.
Silent breakfasts.
Performative date nights.

But it wasn't until she stood in that bedroom doorway, watching the betrayal unfold in real time, that Olivia realized she wasn't sad.

She was free.

The ache didn't come like fire.
It came like air.

Cold. Expansive. Awakening.

She hadn't screamed. She hadn't thrown anything. She hadn't sobbed into the hallway.

Instead, she walked to the fridge and pulled out a bowl of strawberries—the kind Ethan used to steal when he thought she wasn't looking.
She placed them gently into her travel bag.

She didn't pack much. Just her sketchbook. A linen shirt. A soft scarf. The candle from her nightstand.
And the lipstick she hadn't worn since their fifth anniversary.

No wedding ring. No explanation. No second glance.

Only a note left by the lamp on his nightstand, in handwriting he hadn't complimented in years:

I won't fight to be remembered.

Outside, the city was washed in the quiet aftermath of rain.
The pavement shined.
The air tasted different.

She didn't know where she was going.
She just knew it had to be somewhere else.

Somewhere without stale apologies.
Somewhere without silence that echoed with things unsaid.
Somewhere she could breathe without waiting for someone to notice.

This was not a story about betrayal.

This was a story about return.

Not to a man. Not to a home. Not even to a former version of herself.

But to the woman she was before she began folding herself into someone else's comfort.

With her bag on her shoulder and her footsteps soft against the wet pavement, Olivia realized something she wished someone had told her years ago:

You don't have to wait for someone to leave you in order to choose yourself.

You can walk away with your head high and your hands steady.

You can carry your own heart out the door.

And you can do it in silence.

Because sometimes, the loudest thing a woman can ever say... is nothing at all.

Chapter 1

Things That Don't Make a Sound

The click of the door was softer than usual, like the apartment didn't want to be heard.

Olivia stepped in quietly, keys slipping from her fingers into the catch-all bowl by the mirror. She didn't rush. She hadn't meant to arrive early, and she wasn't sure why she hadn't called first. The trip had finished a day ahead of schedule, and she'd convinced herself Ethan would be happy to see her.

Her shoes landed beside the welcome mat. She pressed her palm against the wall, reaching for the switch, but stopped. The apartment was dim. Gentle light leaked from the hallway, pale and golden like late afternoon always gave her. It felt still, too still. Not the peace she craved — the kind that echoes.

She held the strap of her bag against her shoulder and walked through the living room. The carpet felt cool under her bare feet. A small breeze came from the slightly open window above the sink. The scent of vanilla hit her halfway through the room — soft, feminine, expensive. Not the usual sandalwood Ethan wore. Not anything she'd lit before leaving.

Something stirred in her chest. A whisper of warning she didn't want to name.

She passed the framed print by the hallway, the one they picked together two years ago. It was slightly crooked again. She had straightened it before leaving. She always did. Ethan never noticed.

Her hand brushed the edge of the wall as she neared the bedroom. The door was open just enough. A murmur drifted out — not words, but breathy sounds. Intimate. Sinking. Familiar and foreign at the same time.

Her pulse didn't race. It simply slowed.

She pushed the door open with her fingertips.

And the world, as she knew it, exhaled.

Ethan's back was to her.

His hand, tangled in the dark strands of the woman beneath him, moved with the rhythm of someone who'd done this before. Not rushed. Not nervous. Not caught.

Just comfortable.

The woman's laugh was low and airy. She arched against him, her eyes closed, her neck exposed to the ceiling like she belonged there.

Olivia didn't move. Didn't speak.

Time didn't stop. It just fell apart gently, without drama.

She blinked once.

And then again.

Neither of them saw her. Not at first.

The woman's eyes opened mid-moan. She froze.

Ethan turned slowly, as if waking from a dream, and when his gaze landed on Olivia, something cracked in his expression. But it wasn't guilt. It was inconvenience.

"Liv..."

She blinked again.

Still nothing.

Not fury.

Not shame.

Not collapse.

Only silence.

She turned without a word, without a sigh, without a single tremor in her hands. She walked down the hall, one step at a time, like she was moving through water.

The sound of the bedroom door swinging shut behind her was gentle. Final.

She didn't pack everything. Only what mattered.

The linen shirt she loved. Her art sketchbook. A pair of flat sandals. A tube of lip balm. The lavender candle she always kept on her side of the bed. The one Ethan said gave him a headache, but she lit it anyway when she was alone.

She opened the fridge. Reached for the bowl of strawberries she bought the day before her retreat. They were still fresh. She rinsed them one by one under the faucet, fingers steady. They smelled like summer.

She placed the bowl in her tote bag and zipped it shut.

Before she left, she paused at the edge of the bedroom door. She didn't open it. Didn't ask questions. Didn't offer answers.

Instead, she stepped into the study, tore a page from her journal, and scribbled in ink that soaked quickly into the page.

You chose. So now I will, too.

She folded the note once and laid it beside his watch on the nightstand — the one she bought him last Christmas. The one he never wore.

Then she walked out.

The street outside buzzed with life. Cars passed slowly through the residential lanes. A woman jogged by with a golden retriever. A kid skateboarded in lazy zigzags across the opposite sidewalk.

No one noticed her.

She liked that.

Her phone vibrated once. Then again. She didn't check the screen.

She powered it off and dropped it into the deepest part of her bag.

Not out of anger. Not to make a point. She just didn't want to explain herself.

She didn't have the energy to listen to his version of things.

She drove with the windows down.

The air outside smelled like rain, though the sky was clear. Her hair whipped against her cheeks, and for the first time in a long time, she didn't push it away.

She didn't cry.

That surprised her.

Maybe the tears would come later. Or maybe she'd already shed them years ago — in the silences, in the forgotten anniversaries, in the small moments where he left her without ever walking out the door.

There had been so many little endings before this one.

She just hadn't seen them.

Olivia drove until the streetlights blurred.

She parked outside her sister Camille's house and cut the engine. The house was quiet, wrapped in soft yellow porchlight. She texted a simple line: *"Outside. Can I come in?"*

Camille opened the door before Olivia reached the steps.

She didn't ask what happened.

She just hugged her.

And Olivia, for the first time in what felt like years, leaned into someone without needing to pretend she wasn't exhausted.

Later, Camille handed her a blanket and a glass of water. Olivia sat on the guest bed in borrowed pajamas, her tote bag on the floor, the candle beside her on the nightstand, unlit.

She didn't open her sketchbook. Didn't touch the strawberries.

She sat with her knees pulled up to her chest, staring at the wall.

The silence wrapped around her. But it didn't hurt.

It didn't accuse or ache.

It felt like space.

Like room.

Like something waiting.

She whispered into the quiet, just once, just for herself.

"I'm still here."

And for the first time in a long time, that felt like enough.

Chapter 2

The Weight of Still Water

Camille didn't ask any questions.

She opened the front door the moment Olivia texted, stepped aside, and wrapped her arms around her before either of them said a word. Her hug was tight, two arms locked with quiet knowing, like she'd been expecting this day long before Olivia had.

Olivia didn't cry. She didn't stiffen either. She just stood there in her sister's arms, letting herself be held for the first time in what felt like months.

"I made chamomile," Camille said gently, pulling back just enough to look her in the face. "Come in. You can talk when you're ready. Or not at all."

The smell of warm honey and herbs wrapped around her the moment she crossed the threshold. Camille's home was always like that — full of softness, nothing loud, nothing sharp. Even the walls were painted in pale, warm tones. Like safety.

Olivia slipped off her shoes. Her fingers brushed the buckle of her bag, but she didn't open it yet. She wasn't ready to touch the things inside.

The guest room was smaller than she remembered. The bed was made with a knitted throw at the edge, a candle unlit on the dresser, and a folded sweatshirt she'd left behind months ago. The kind Ethan hated — the one with paint stains down the sleeves.

She pulled it on and sat down slowly, like the room might disappear if she moved too fast.

Camille set the tea down on the side table.

"I'll leave you alone," she said softly, pausing at the door. "Just knock if you need anything. Or sleep. Or silence."

Olivia gave her a small nod. No words.

The door clicked shut.

She stared at the tea until the steam faded.

Then she reached for her bag.

Inside was the linen shirt, the candle, the lip balm, and the sketchbook. She set them on the bed like small artifacts. Her eyes landed last on the bowl of strawberries, still nestled carefully in the corner.

She lifted one out. It was perfect. Bright, plump, fragrant. She held it between her fingers for a long time before placing it back into the bowl.

She didn't eat it.

She just needed to know it was still whole.

Night came gently.

She didn't hear Camille move through the house. Didn't notice the change in the light until the lamp by the bed glowed yellow across the blanket.

Olivia lay down, but her body stayed awake. Her eyes didn't close. Her thoughts didn't race either. They floated. They swayed. Like ripples in a lake, moving without destination.

She thought about the way Ethan looked at her when he realized she was standing in the doorway. Not panicked. Not ashamed. Just... caught.

She thought about the way he used to reach for her in the mornings, eyes still heavy with sleep, pulling her close before the day stole him away.

She thought about the way that stopped months ago.

Maybe longer.

Around midnight, she finally lit the candle.

The room smelled like lavender and something else she couldn't name. It wasn't peace, but it wasn't pain either.

She opened the sketchbook.

The first page was blank.

She stared at it, pencil in hand, not drawing. Just holding space.

Her fingers trembled, not from emotion but from stillness. Like they hadn't been used for their true purpose in too long.

Eventually, she drew a line. Then another. Nothing recognizable. Just movement. Flow. A way to remind her body that it could still make something.

She wrote under it in small, precise letters:

Everything is still here. It just hurts in different places now.

The next morning came slowly.

Camille had left toast and marmalade on the counter with a note that read, *"I took the kids to school. Stay as long as you need."*

Olivia ate two bites. The taste didn't reach her.

She stared out the kitchen window at the backyard. The swing set they used to play on when they were little stood crooked now, one rope fraying at the edge.

She wondered how long it had been like that.

She hadn't noticed before.

Camille came back just after ten. She didn't ask about Ethan.

She sat across the table with a second cup of tea and said, "I'm glad you're here."

Olivia nodded. "I should've come sooner."

"You came when you were ready."

Olivia traced the rim of her mug. "It didn't feel like anything. Walking in. Seeing him."

"You were numb."

"No." Her voice was quiet. "I was finished."

Camille didn't respond with words. She reached across the table and squeezed her hand. That was enough.

That afternoon, Olivia took a shower and washed her hair. She watched water run down her arms, the scent of lavender shampoo rising with the steam. She wrapped herself in Camille's soft robe and stood by the mirror.

For the first time, she looked at herself. Really looked.

Her eyes were tired, but not broken. Her mouth was soft. No sharp lines.

She looked like someone who had nothing left to explain.

And that, strangely, felt like freedom.

Later that evening, she stood by the window in the guest room. Outside, the sky turned amber. Light filtered through the glass and touched everything in gold.

She pulled her sketchbook into her arms and held it there, pressed close to her chest like a promise.

Ethan hadn't called again.

She hadn't turned her phone back on.

The silence was no longer heavy.

It had begun to feel like still water — not empty, just calm.

And in its quiet, she was beginning to hear herself again.

Chapter 3

Rooms with No Soundtrack

She hadn't planned to drive past the old building.

But there it was—tucked into the corner of Maple and Fifth—like a ghost waiting to be remembered. Their first apartment. The one with no dishwasher, one flickering lightbulb in the hallway, and floors that creaked in protest every time someone walked through the door.

She parked across the street, engine idling, hands resting on the wheel. The red awning was gone. New mailbox. A sleeker doorbell. But the bones were the same. She could still picture the mismatched curtains they hung in the kitchen, the thrift store table with one uneven leg, and the corner where their first Christmas tree leaned tipsily toward the wall.

The memory didn't slam into her. It drifted in like steam from a forgotten kettle—slow, insistent, and thick with ache: their first night inside, pizza boxes stacked on the counter, music from Ethan's phone echoing through the empty space, her laughter curled around his sweatshirt as they danced barefoot across blueprints of a life they hadn't yet smudged. They didn't have a bed yet. Just a mattress on the floor and an old lamp that flickered when it rained.

That version of them was long gone. But Olivia couldn't quite look away.

She turned off the ignition and sat still.

Some things don't break loudly. They just lose color.

Back at Camille's house, the quiet pressed in closer than usual. The hallway dimmed by drawn blinds, smelled faintly of lavender and something simmering on the stove. Olivia stepped into the kitchen and stood still for a moment. Then she moved.

She emptied and rearranged the pantry. Alphabetized the spices. Scrubbed the microwave until the buttons gleamed. Tightened the loose handle on the cupboard. Not out of duty. Out of ache.

Camille leaned into the doorway, barefoot and observant.

"You don't have to earn your space here," she said.

Olivia didn't turn. "I know. I just needed something to hold."

Camille nodded. Her silence said: *I understand.*

Later, Olivia retreated to the guest room. The lavender candle flickered on the windowsill, casting shaky shapes onto the comforter. She sat cross-legged on the bed, sketchpad on her knees, pencil between fingers smudged faintly with soot and oil.

She flipped through the pages. Her drawings weren't masterpieces. They weren't meant to be. Faces in fragments. A door slightly ajar. A bowl of strawberries under a cracked window. They were memory and muscle. Proof that her hands still moved.

One page stopped her.

A hand, half-drawn, reaching off the paper. She didn't remember sketching it. But the caption beneath was hers:

Wanting doesn't mean belonging.

She stared at it for a long time. Not sad. Just still.

Later that night, digging through her travel bag for an old poem she wanted to copy, she pulled out a slim paperback. As she flipped through its final pages, something slipped free and landed softly on the blanket.

A folded sketch.

Her breath hitched.

She unfolded it slowly, the way you open a letter you're not ready to read but can't let go of. Ethan's handwriting. His sketching style—light strokes, unpracticed but careful.

It was her. Sitting on the couch in her old gray sweatshirt, knees tucked under her, reading. Hair loose. Expression soft. No makeup. No pose. Just her, as she was.

Below it, he had written:

Even when she doesn't know it, she saves me.

The ache didn't roar. It hummed.

Her chest tightened. Her throat constricted.

Was I ever truly invisible?

A single sharp breath. Then another.

She folded the sketch in half and then in half again. Not to destroy it. Not to save it. Just to contain it.

She placed it inside the back of her sketchpad and whispered:

"It wasn't enough."

The words didn't hurt. They steadied her.

In the morning, Camille made cinnamon tea and set a cup beside her on the kitchen table.

"I heard you moving around last night."

"I found something," Olivia said. "A sketch Ethan drew of me. I don't even remember ever seeing it before."

Camille tilted her head, gently curious.

Olivia looked up. "He saw me. Once. But only when I wasn't asking to be seen."

Camille nodded. "That doesn't mean he knew what he was seeing."

"I think I'm just starting to understand the difference between being looked at and being known."

Camille's hand reached across the table and found Olivia's wrist. "And which one do you deserve?"

"Both," Olivia said. "But only from someone who offers it without needing to be reminded."

That afternoon, Olivia wandered into the little art supply store near the bookstore. She picked up charcoal pencils and a journal with a soft leather cover. Her fingers ran across thick paper and glass jars of pigment like they were made of memory.

It wasn't about needing tools. It was about reclaiming the right to want beauty.

Back at the house, she cleared the desk in the guest room. Arranged her tools in a line—pencils, sharpener, sketchpad, candle, mug of tea.

She started to draw. Slowly. Carefully.

A woman standing in front of a window. Her shadow stretching behind her, a vine curling along the sill. One hand pressed to the glass. The other, open.

She titled it: *Choosing Stillness.*

That evening, Camille found her on the back porch, mug in hand, Ethan's old hoodie wrapped around her like a memory she wasn't trying to forget—but no longer needed to wear for warmth.

"You feel heavier today," Camille said.

"I'm tired. Not just my body. My spirit." Olivia's voice was a low rasp. "Like I've been living in pieces too long."

"Then maybe it's time to live whole. Even if you're still figuring out what that means."

Olivia turned toward the horizon.

"I don't know who I am out there."

Camille's reply was quiet. "Then start here. One breath at a time. One tea. One sketch. No rush."

The chimes clinked in the wind. Dusk turned the edges of the sky violet.

Neither said another word. And it was enough.

That night, Olivia dreamed she was painting the walls of the old apartment. But instead of restoring it, each stroke erased something: a slammed door, a night of silence, the sound of her own voice asking, *Do you still love me?*

When she woke, the sky was bruised with early light. She grabbed her sketchpad and wrote in soft pencil:

Some silences are wounds. Others are wombs.

Then she turned the page.

And drew again.

Chapter 4

The Room Where I Didn't Beg

Olivia hadn't planned to meet him.

She didn't rehearse what she would say. There were no mirror monologues or imaginary scenarios, no list of things he deserved to hear. She didn't even know why she replied to his message. It just happened. Like a shift in the tide. Like a door she hadn't locked swinging open on its own.

The café was quiet. Neutral. A place without history. That was important. No ghosts here.

She arrived five minutes early and sat at the table near the window. Light poured through the glass, gentle and forgiving. She kept her hands in her lap and stared at the swirl of milk in her tea.

When Ethan walked in, she knew it was him before she looked up.

His presence still carried weight, but it didn't knock the air out of her like it used to. It didn't fill her chest or twist her stomach. It just existed. There. Across from her.

He sat down slowly, like he wasn't sure he had the right.

Olivia raised her eyes and met his without flinching.

"You look good," he said, voice low. "Healthy."

She didn't reply. She didn't smile either.

He cleared his throat. "Thank you for agreeing to meet me."

Still, she said nothing.

There was power in that, and not the performative kind. The kind that said: *I owe you nothing, but I'm here anyway.*

He shifted in his seat, reached for the napkin, folded it, unfolded it again. His wedding ring was gone. She hadn't expected it to still be there, but seeing his bare finger felt... final.

"I know you don't want to hear excuses," he began.

"I don't," she answered. Calm. Even. Not cruel.

He blinked. "Okay."

He leaned back, and for a second, he looked like the man she used to know — but only a second.

"I just wanted to see you. To explain... something. Anything."

She picked up her tea. Sipped once. Set it down.

"You don't need to explain," she said. "Not for me. Maybe for you."

Ethan looked away.

Outside, someone walked a dog with a red leash. A cyclist drifted past in slow motion. The world continued. That felt important.

"I miss you," he said.

Olivia nodded once. "I don't."

He opened his mouth, closed it again. The weight of her words landed between them like a stone dropped into water.

"I miss us."

"There hasn't been an 'us' in a long time."

Ethan looked down. "I made a mistake."

"No," she said, voice even. "You made a choice."

His shoulders slumped.

She didn't hate him. That would've been easier. Cleaner. But she didn't feel pity either.

What she felt was understanding. The kind that didn't require forgiveness.

"I don't expect you to take me back," he said after a long silence.

She tilted her head slightly. "Good. Because I won't."

"I just wanted... to talk. To apologize. Properly."

"Apologies are only useful if they change something."

He looked up at her, eyes glassy. "I never stopped loving you."

She held his gaze. "You stopped showing it."

A beat passed. Then another.

"I loved you the best I could."

Olivia's voice didn't rise. "And I accepted less than I deserved for longer than I should have. That doesn't make either of us noble."

She leaned forward, not out of anger, but clarity.

"I didn't leave because you slept with someone else," she said. "I left because I was tired of being invisible. I left because you only touched me when it was convenient. Because I spent months shrinking into the spaces you stopped looking."

"I didn't know—"

"You did," she said. "You just didn't care enough to change."

That silence again.

This time, it felt like the truth had emptied the room.

Ehan looked older than she remembered. Not in his face, but in his posture. Like shame had worn him down in the places she couldn't reach.

"I never wanted to hurt you."

"But you did."

He nodded, slowly, painfully.

"I just want to know if there's any part of you that... still believes in us."

Olivia smiled — soft, almost kind.

"There's a part of me that still believes in who we were. But who we were is gone."

Ethan looked away.

"And I love who I'm becoming more than I miss what we used to be."

She stood up.

He stayed seated.

No dramatic exit. No walking away with a flourish. Just a woman who had already left long before she stood.

"Take care of yourself, Ethan."

He didn't respond. Only nodded, lips pressed together.

She walked past the counter, through the door, and out into the sun. It was warmer now. The wind had softened.

She breathed in.

Not relief.

Not sadness.

Something cleaner.

She didn't cry when she got back to Camille's.

Instead, she changed into her sweatshirt, pulled her hair into a messy knot, and lit her lavender candle.

She opened her sketchpad and began a new page.

This time, it was a doorway. Cracked open. Light spilling through. A figure in shadow turning away.

At the bottom, she wrote:

I didn't lose love. I let go of what was no longer love at all.

Chapter 5

The Art of Coming Back Slowly

The sun filtered through the curtains in streaks of gold.

Olivia opened her eyes without urgency. The ceiling above her was unfamiliar, but no longer strange. The soft hum of the neighborhood seeped through the window — distant traffic, a barking dog, someone's wind chimes dancing with the breeze.

She exhaled into the quiet.

No alarm. No calendar reminder. No voice in the other room expecting her to be anywhere else but here.

She pulled the blanket higher for a moment, resting in the weight of stillness.

This was the first morning in years she woke up without adjusting herself to someone else's presence.

And that was something worth noticing.

She padded into the kitchen, barefoot, the floor cool against her skin. Camille had already left a note.

"Took the kids to the dentist. Help yourself to the garden strawberries — they're ripe."

She smiled.

The garden had been Camille's therapy. Lavender, thyme, two rows of tomatoes, and one small patch of strawberries. Nothing perfect, just alive.

Olivia walked outside, arms wrapped around herself, and let the late morning sun warm her shoulders. The air was fresh. Earthy. Honest.

She crouched by the strawberry bed, brushing her fingers across the leaves. The fruit was red and plump, still damp with dew. She picked three gently, one at a time, and sat on the low stone wall nearby.

She ate slowly.

Bite by bite.

Juice on her fingers. Sweetness on her tongue.

It wasn't just a strawberry. It was proof of life.

Something quiet, growing, and giving — even after neglect.

Later, she returned inside and opened her sketchpad.

She sat cross-legged by the window, the charcoal pencil loose between her fingers. There was no plan. No pressure. Just space. Just breath.

The page filled itself — gentle curves, soft shadows. A hand cupping light. A window half-open. A candle dripping wax beside an empty teacup.

Her art had never been for show. Ethan once suggested she post her sketches online, maybe sell them. She never did. Not because they weren't good enough — but because they were hers.

They were the only place she'd never shrunk.

By mid-afternoon, Olivia took a walk to the nearby bookstore. It was small, family-owned, and smelled like pages and old leather. The woman at the counter had silver hair twisted into a knot and smiled without asking questions.

She wandered the aisles slowly. Her fingers traced spines. Poetry. Travel. Art.

In the back corner, she found a slim paperback — *The Art of Being Alone Without Feeling Lost*. She flipped it open to a random page:

"Sometimes, solitude is not an absence of love, but the presence of self."

She bought it without hesitation.

That evening, Camille joined her on the porch steps.

They shared a bowl of pasta and two glasses of wine. The kids were upstairs, whispering behind closed doors, laughter tucked behind their stories.

Olivia told Camille about the strawberries. The bookstore. The sketch she'd drawn.

Camille smiled, not because it was dramatic or impressive, but because it was movement.

"I like this version of you," she said gently.

"I don't even know who she is yet."

"Then take your time getting to know her. She's been waiting."

They watched the sky turn from blue to lavender. One of the kids shouted something through the window. Camille laughed and stood.

Olivia stayed behind.

The breeze kissed her face. The stars began to show themselves in small flickers.

She thought about Ethan, but not in longing.

She thought about herself, and this time — without shame.

She pulled her phone from her pocket, turned it over in her hands, and finally opened the voice message he left a few days ago.

It played quietly, his voice softer than she remembered.

"Liv... I don't know where to start. I messed up. I know that. And I don't expect you to forgive me. I just... I miss us. I miss you. Please call me back. Or don't. I just needed to say it."

She deleted it.

Not out of anger. But because she no longer needed to carry it.

Back inside, she placed her sketchpad on her pillow and turned off the light.

The candle flickered beside her.

She lay on her side and whispered into the quiet:

"I'm still here."

Not broken.

Not whole.

Just... here.

And that, finally, was enough.

Chapter 6

Women Who Don't Say Everything

The flyer wasn't flashy. Just cream-colored cardstock pinned to a corkboard beside the café, nestled between a piano lesson notice and a missing cat poster. The corners curled slightly, like it had been waiting for her longer than she knew.

Art & Mindfulness Workshop – Mondays 10 a.m.
No experience needed.
A space to create, feel, and breathe.

Olivia didn't take the whole flyer. She tore the corner with the email address and slid it into her coat pocket, careful not to wrinkle it. A fragile yes she hadn't said aloud yet, but one she was willing to carry.

She wasn't ready to be seen. Not completely. But there was something about the words—*no experience needed*—that felt like an invitation, not just to draw, but to show up. Quietly. Flawed. Still in progress.

That night, she sat on the edge of the guest bed, her sketchpad untouched beside her. The lavender candle flickered on the nightstand, and Camille's house settled into silence around her.

She opened her phone and typed the message without letting herself hesitate.

Hi, I'd like to attend your Monday class. Is there space for one more?

The reply arrived by morning:

Hi Olivia,
Absolutely. Just bring yourself. All supplies provided.
Warmly, Sofia

That single sentence settled into her chest like a welcome.

The workshop met in a converted sunroom attached to an old bungalow two blocks from Camille's. The windows stretched nearly from floor to ceiling, veiled with soft linen curtains that filtered the light like morning fog.

Six chairs formed a loose circle on the hardwood floor. In the back were open shelves stacked with art supplies—pastels, graphite, watercolor trays, acrylic tubes, brushes worn at the ends, and jars filled with rinsed-out jam spoons repurposed as palette knives.

No tables. No mirrors. No name tags.

Just space.

Sofia was the kind of woman who smiled with her eyes first. She greeted Olivia with a warmth that didn't intrude.

"You found us."

"I did."

"You're right on time."

There were no introductions. No icebreakers. No questions about where you worked or why you came.

The women arrived gradually. One with gray-streaked curls and a handwoven shawl. Another who looked no older than twenty, her hoodie sleeves pulled over her fists. A woman in lipstick the color of dried roses, who walked with confidence but spoke softly.

They settled into the circle. Sofia lit a stick of incense—something earthy and grounding—and placed it in a small ceramic bowl in the center of the floor.

"We don't make art here to impress anyone," she said, voice low and kind. "We make it to listen."

They began.

Sofia didn't instruct. She invited.

"Close your eyes," she said. "Notice where your hands feel heavy. Ask them what they want to hold."

Olivia closed her eyes. Her hands tingled slightly, nervous but awake. When she opened them again, she reached for charcoal. The weight of it felt real in her palm—smoky and honest.

Shapes formed before she named them. A cracked window. A tree bending toward light. A woman with her back turned, half disappearing into the paper. Olivia didn't plan the lines. She followed them.

By the end of the session, her fingers were smudged black. Her breath, steadier.

Sofia walked by and placed a folded cloth on her lap.

"You don't have to explain it," she said. "But your hands told the truth today."

Olivia nodded. "I forgot how much they knew."

The next Monday, Olivia arrived early. She helped arrange the brushes into mason jars, refilled the rinse cups, and adjusted the chairs slightly so they opened more toward the center.

Sofia noticed but didn't comment. She just smiled.

That day, a new woman came in. Late twenties, maybe. Hair knotted into a bun that looked like it had been twisted up in the dark. She held her shoulders like armor.

She sat near the window, clutching her lapboard as though someone might take it away.

Olivia approached quietly. Offered her a clean page and a half-used stick of pastel.

"You don't have to know what to draw. You just have to begin."

The woman didn't answer. But by the end of the hour, slow spirals had bloomed across her page—light gray, dusty rose, a smudge of green near the corner.

Later, as the others cleaned up, Olivia paused beside her.

"That's enough," she said gently.

The woman didn't look up. But her hands relaxed slightly.

Sometimes healing doesn't declare itself. It just takes up a little more space than yesterday.

That evening, Camille found Olivia at the kitchen counter, sketchpad open. Two hands took shape on the page—one open, one tentative. On the windowsill above them sat a single unlit candle.

"You're glowing," Camille said.

Olivia smirked. "I'm dusty."

"Dusty and glowing," Camille said, sipping from a chipped mug. "Works for me."

Olivia turned the page. Drew a faceless figure wrapped in fabric, standing in the middle of a windy field.

"Today, Sofia asked us to draw anger."

Camille raised an eyebrow. "And what did you draw?"

Olivia hesitated. "A window. And a man sleeping next to it. Peacefully. Like nothing had ever happened."

Camille didn't speak.

"I think I was angrier at myself. For staying quiet. For staying long after the quiet had become a wound."

Camille placed her mug down. "You're not the only woman who's tried to make silence feel like safety."

"No," Olivia said. "But I don't want to keep being one."

That night, Olivia couldn't sleep. She sat on the floor of the guest room, legs tucked beneath her, sketchpad resting on her thighs.

She traced slow lines—repeating shapes: windows, doors, mirrors. Things that either open or reflect. Things that demand presence.

She wrote beneath one drawing:

Some women rebuild quietly. That doesn't make their strength smaller.

She stared. Crossed out "quietly." Wrote above it: *deliberately.*

Some women rebuild deliberately.

That felt more true.

The next week, during class, Sofia passed around small mirrors. "Look," she said. "And draw what your eyes say."

Olivia's heart stuttered.

She stared at her reflection. Not the shape of her face, but the way her eyes held fatigue and fire in equal measure. She began to sketch—not the contour of her jaw, but the slope of her gaze, the quiet steel.

Tears welled unexpectedly. She blinked them back.

She didn't want to draw herself as she had been.

She didn't want to draw the woman she'd been. She wanted to capture the one still forming—unfinished, but finally her own.

That night, she titled the drawing: *Becoming.*

And beneath it, she wrote:

I'm still becoming. But this time, I'm looking myself in the eye.

Chapter 7

The Shape of Somewhere Safe

The word "home" used to come with coordinates.

A familiar door. A man's voice in the hallway. The weight of shared keys and shared bills and shared silences.

But Olivia no longer believed that four walls made anything sacred.

She had been in Camille's guest room for three weeks. Long enough for the lavender candle to melt halfway down. Long enough to forget what it felt like to make space for someone else's moods. Long enough to start wondering — not about going back, but about *where to go from here.*

She wasn't lost.

But she wasn't settled either.

Somewhere in between was its own kind of wilderness.

She sat on the back steps of Camille's house, mug of tea in hand, watching the morning spill into the garden. Bees darted near the basil, the air thick with summer. A robin pecked near the lavender bush, its head tilting like it knew something she didn't.

She pulled her knees to her chest and took a slow sip.

She didn't miss Ethan.
Not the real Ethan.
But sometimes she missed the *idea* of a future that was already planned.

Life without blueprints felt too quiet some days.

But quiet was better than being muted.

Camille came out in a soft robe, barefoot, holding her own mug.

"Morning," she said gently.

Olivia nodded. "It's beautiful today."

Camille glanced at her. "You thinking about moving out?"

Olivia blinked. "Do I need to?"

"No," Camille said with a soft smile. "But I know the look. You've been dreaming of something else."

"I don't even know what it looks like."

"Then maybe start by asking what it *feels* like."

Later that afternoon, Olivia took a walk.
No destination. Just forward.

She passed a row of old houses, each one with chipped paint and creaking porches. Each one holding a story she'd never know. She paused at one with ivy climbing the sides, windows flung open, music floating out — something soft and old, maybe jazz.

She smiled.

It was the kind of place she would've ignored before. Too worn. Too imperfect.

Now it felt... honest.

By evening, she found herself back at the bookstore.
The same woman with silver hair greeted her, this time with recognition.

"You're becoming a regular."

"I think I'm trying to build a life out of paper and stillness."

The woman chuckled. "Could do worse."

Olivia wandered through the shelves, stopping this time in the journals section.

She picked one with a linen cover and blank pages. No lines. No rules.

She held it against her chest for a moment before walking to the counter.

Back at Camille's, she spread out her sketchpad and the new journal on the bed. She didn't write yet. Just opened to the first page and stared.

She didn't want to tell the story of what happened.

She wanted to tell the story of what was *beginning*.

So she wrote:

A home doesn't have to be a place.
It can be a morning.
A person.
A moment where you choose yourself completely.

The next day, Camille drove her to see a small cottage outside of town.
Not a formal viewing. Just something she thought Olivia should see.

"It's probably too quiet for you," Camille said, handing her the keys. "But just... take a look."

It sat at the end of a gravel path, hidden behind an arch of trees. Two windows in front. A small porch with chipped railings. A wooden door painted faded blue.

The garden had long since given up. Weeds. Wildflowers. A stubborn rosemary bush in the corner.

Inside was empty. Echoing. Dusty.

But Olivia stood in the doorway and closed her eyes.

And for the first time in months, she imagined her things inside.

Her drawings on the wall.
A candle on the kitchen counter.
A bowl of strawberries near the sink.
No silence she had to tiptoe around.
No shadows of someone else's absence.

Just space. Just choice.

Just her.

Camille leaned against the doorframe behind her.

"You'd need to fix the porch. Probably replace a few windows."

Olivia turned slowly. "I don't mind doing the work."

Camille smiled. "I know."

That night, Olivia didn't sleep much.
She lay in bed staring at the ceiling, her heart quiet but alert.

She wasn't afraid.
She wasn't running.
She wasn't lost.

She was, for the first time, *ready*.

In her sketchpad, she drew the porch.

Not as it was, but as it could be.

A soft chair. A candle on a small table. A figure sitting with her knees tucked under her, not waiting — just resting.

She wrote below it:

I don't need to be rescued.
I just need a place to begin again.
And I choose here.

Chapter 8

Quiet Things That Begin to Grow

The key turned with effort.

The door creaked open into stillness, the kind that felt untouched by time. Light slanted through the dusty windows in narrow beams. The floor groaned softly beneath her feet, and the scent of forgotten wood and something earthy hung in the air.

Olivia stepped inside slowly, the way one walks into a church or a memory.

This place had no history with her. No echoes of laughter or arguments. No picture frames marking anniversaries. No drawers filled with love letters or receipts of disappointment.

It was blank.

And for the first time in her life, blank felt like hope.

The first night in the cottage, she slept on a borrowed mattress on the floor. One pillow. Two blankets. The lavender candle flickering on the windowsill.

No curtains yet. Just the moonlight washing in, silver and forgiving.

She didn't unpack fully. She didn't need to. A bowl of strawberries sat on the crate beside her mattress. Her sketchbook rested beneath it.

She slept in soft silence.
No footsteps in another room.
No alarms set.
No man turning over with his back to her dreams.

Just breath. Just stillness.

And when she woke in the middle of the night, heart calm, she smiled to herself in the dark.

She was alone.
And safe.
And finally, not waiting to be chosen.

The mornings came slowly.

She began with toast, jam, and herbal tea.
Soft music on her phone, just loud enough to warm the

corners of the room.

She swept the floors, cleaned the windows, and opened the front door to let the light in.

Each movement felt like an agreement.

Yes, I want to be here.
Yes, I will try again.
Yes, I'm still learning how to be mine.

Her art corner took shape by the second week. A small desk, secondhand but sturdy, faced the front window. She placed a vase with dried lavender on the edge, next to a jar of charcoal sticks and a set of new watercolors she had bought with no guilt this time.

She didn't draw for hours.

Just enough to remember her hands were capable of making beauty again.

Sometimes she painted a leaf, other times an empty chair, and once, a woman in profile whose expression said everything Olivia hadn't found the words for yet.

She didn't need to post it.
Didn't need feedback or approval.

It wasn't for the world.
It was for her return.

By the third week, she planted lavender in the garden.

The soil was stubborn. Dry in some places. Rich in others.

She knelt beside the rosemary bush that had outlived its neglect and whispered, "I get it."

She dug with her hands, nails caked with earth, knees bruised from stone. It didn't matter. Every root she pressed into the soil felt like a vow.

Something will grow here.
Even if it takes time.
Even if no one else sees it.

Sofia visited one afternoon with a tin of herbal tea and a loaf of cinnamon bread wrapped in cloth.

They sat on the front step, shoes off, backs resting against the faded railing Olivia still hadn't repaired.

"You look different," Sofia said.

Olivia smiled. "Freer?"

"Fuller."

She tapped her finger against the rim of her mug. "I think I'm starting to fill in my own absence."

They shared a few slices of bread and let the silence stretch.

Sofia reached into her bag and pulled out a small jar.

"For your windowsill," she said, placing it in Olivia's hand.

Inside was a single strawberry plant, its stem fragile, but its leaves bright.

"It's young," Sofia said. "But it's trying."

Olivia's throat tightened.

"Just like me."

That night, Olivia wrote in her journal:

I'm not rebuilding what was.
I'm building what never had the chance to exist.
A home that isn't defined by who's in it.
But how I feel inside it.

Days passed gently.

She fixed the squeaky back door, sanded the porch railings, planted basil and thyme beside the lavender.

She hung wind chimes outside the kitchen window and let their soft notes break the quiet just enough to feel alive.

At night, she sat on the floor with a cup of tea and let her eyes wander over her drawings, her garden plans, her quiet joy.

The loneliness wasn't gone. But it was quieter.
Like a background hum instead of a scream.
Like a soft ache you learn to stretch around.

One morning, she stood barefoot in the garden, the strawberry plant from Sofia blooming beside her. Her hands smelled of rosemary. Her sweatshirt was speckled with paint and soil.

She smiled at nothing in particular.

"I think I'm okay."

Not perfect.

Not whole.

But planted.
And growing.

Chapter 9

When the Leaves Begin to Listen

The first cool breeze came quietly — a whisper against her shoulder as she watered the lavender outside.

Olivia paused, pitcher in hand, and looked up at the sky. It was paler than it had been all summer. The kind of pale that meant something was shifting — not gone, not yet, but in motion.

The air smelled different too.

Less sugar. More wood.

She stood barefoot on the back porch and watched the wind stir the trees. The rosemary bush bent slightly. A few petals floated down from the early blooms. Nothing loud. Nothing dramatic.

But she felt it.

Autumn was arriving.
And something inside her was softening with it.

She spent the afternoon rearranging the bookshelf. Not out of necessity, but because it felt like an act of presence.

Poetry to the top.
Journals to the bottom.
Her favorite art books right in the middle, near the candle and the plant that still hadn't bloomed but hadn't died either.

She made tea. Lit incense. Played an instrumental playlist that didn't demand attention.

And for the first time in a long time, she didn't crave distraction.

She let the quiet stay.

By early evening, she opened her journal and began to write.

Not about Ethan.
Not about what she had lost.

But about the wind.
The rosemary.

The way her fingers had stopped trembling every time she picked up a pencil.

Her words flowed like breath.

She didn't force them.
She followed them.

They didn't look like a novel or a memoir. They looked like pieces. Observations. Fragments of feeling that didn't need to form a whole to be honest.

The next morning, she walked to the market at the edge of town.

The air was crisp. Her sweatshirt sleeves pulled down over her hands. Her hair tucked into a loose braid.

She passed a mother holding a toddler. A man selling baked goods. A woman arranging dahlias in mason jars.

There was music playing from a small speaker near the coffee stall. Something old, something mellow.

She bought pears, honey, a bundle of sunflowers, and a notebook with a green linen cover.

When the woman at the stall smiled at her and said, "Looks like you're stocking up for something beautiful," Olivia didn't deflect.

She simply replied, "I think I am."

Back home, she placed the sunflowers in a glass jar and sat by the window with the green notebook in her lap.

On the first page, she wrote:

This is not about what happened.
This is about what is possible now.

She closed the cover and held it in her hands.

It felt warm. Real. Her own.

That night, she dreamed of the cottage — but it wasn't hers.

It was someone else's.

She was just passing through, barefoot, hands dusted with soil. The house was filled with light and other women. They were laughing, painting, sipping from teacups. No one asked where she had come from. They just nodded. They made room.

She woke up smiling.

Sofia stopped by with another plant. This one was a delicate vine, curling at the edges of its terracotta pot.

"It doesn't like too much sun," she said. "But if you talk to it, it grows toward your voice."

Olivia laughed. "So it listens?"

"More than most people do."

They sat on the porch drinking spiced tea and listening to the wind chimes.

"You ever think of writing something bigger?" Sofia asked gently.

Olivia shrugged. "I used to."

"Maybe now is the time."

"I don't even know where to begin."

"Start where you are," Sofia said, "and write like no one's asking for a beginning."

In the evening, Olivia stood in her garden, hands buried in the soil, and looked up at the trees. A few leaves had turned gold. One drifted down and landed on her sleeve.

She smiled.

Not everything needed to be loud to matter.

Inside, she lit the candle, pulled on her sweater, and opened the green notebook again.

She didn't write a title.
She didn't label it "Chapter One."
She didn't outline the story.

She just began.

Chapter 10

The Quiet Before Goodbye

The cottage was still when she woke.

Light crept in through the half-open curtain, catching dust in golden streaks. Outside, the wind stirred the chimes, soft as lullabies. The garden was damp from the night's rain, its earth rich with a scent that only belonged to mornings like this.

Olivia lay there for a moment, listening to the stillness.

No rush.
No plan.
Just the soft echo of a woman who had finally stopped running from herself.

She rose and pulled on her sweater — the one with a frayed sleeve and a faint ink blot near the wrist. Her favorite.

In the kitchen, she boiled water, steeped tea, and cut a pear. The knife moved slowly through the flesh, its sweetness rising in the quiet air.

The green notebook waited on the table beside a single sunflower that had dried but still stood with elegance. She didn't open it yet.

First, she stepped outside.

The air smelled like pine and smoke from someone's chimney down the lane. The garden shimmered with dew. A few rosemary sprigs had started to flower, their scent rising whenever she brushed past them.

The strawberry plant Sofia had given her now held two small fruits. One ripened, the other still white.

She crouched beside it, gently touching the stem.

"You're doing fine," she whispered.

She picked the ripe berry and brought it to her lips.

The flavor was quiet. Gentle. Like something that had waited its whole life for this exact moment.

Back inside, she carried her tea to the window and opened the notebook.

The page from yesterday stared back at her:

This is not about what happened.
This is about what is possible now.

She turned to the next one.

No longer afraid of blank spaces.

She wrote:

Today, I didn't wait for peace.
I made it.
With water, and breath, and strawberries in the
morning light.
And I didn't have to earn it.
I just had to choose it.

The kettle whistled. The wind passed. The day unfolded slowly, like a poem that didn't need to rhyme.

She cleaned the kitchen.

Answered a letter from Camille's daughter.

Sketched a row of teacups on the back of a bill envelope.

And when she lit the candle on her desk — the last one in her drawer — she didn't feel nostalgic. Just present.

Ethan hadn't contacted her again.

She hadn't looked him up. Hadn't checked social media. Not from restraint, but because he simply... didn't live in her anymore.

His absence was not a wound.

It was a cleared path.

In the afternoon, she found herself sorting through the folded letters and sketches she had tucked in a box — fragments of herself that used to feel like losses.

She didn't cry.

She smiled at the handwriting.
At the paper soft from being touched too many times.
At the lines that once tried to make sense of her grief.

She took out one sketch — a candle and a window, drawn in her darkest days — and pinned it above her desk.

She no longer needed to explain where it came from.

It was part of the architecture now.

She spent the rest of the day planting a small patch of calendula. The soil was ready. The seeds light in her hand. No rush. No pressure.

Just the quiet promise that something else would bloom.

At dusk, she brought out a second cup of tea.

Not for anyone else.

Just because she could.

Because having room for another — even when no one filled it — was its own kind of healing.

She watched the sky dim, her sweater sleeves pulled low, the candle still flickering in the window behind her.

The wind brushed her face like a question she no longer feared answering.

In her final journal entry that night, she wrote:

I didn't lose myself.
I simply returned.
Not with noise.
But with breath.
With soil beneath my nails and sunlight on my shoulder.
With art no one had to see and love that didn't need to be earned.
And when I said goodbye — not to him, but to the version of me who waited to be chosen —

I heard something beautiful in the silence.
It sounded like home.

Epilogue

The Morning After the Ending

It rained the night before.

Not loudly. Just enough to leave the ground soft and the windows streaked with tiny trails of silver. Olivia stood barefoot by the open door, her sweater sleeves pulled over her wrists, hands wrapped around a warm mug.

The rosemary glistened.
The soil smelled alive.
The wind moved like breath.

There were no phone calls.
No old names flickering across her screen.
No questions left unanswered.

Only this:

The quiet.

The candle.
The morning.

She had learned that healing doesn't come in milestones.

It doesn't wait for applause or clarity.

It happens in the way your body stops flinching when you hear your own name.

It happens in the way you begin to sit inside your silence — not because you've given up on being heard, but because you finally believe in your own voice.

She stepped outside and pressed her heel gently into the earth. The porch creaked as she passed. A single strawberry hung from the plant, ripe and perfect.

She didn't pluck it.

She let it stay.

Some things, she had learned, were meant to be admired — not possessed.

Back inside, she opened her journal and drew a house.

Not hers.
Not Ethan's.
Just a space with an open window, a steaming mug on the ledge, and a sky painted in quiet colors.

Below it, she wrote:

"The goodbye wasn't the end.
It was the quiet that gave me back my beginning."

She closed the notebook.

No need to write more today.

She had said what she needed to say.

To the silence.
To herself.

And for once, that was enough.

Printed in Dunstable, United Kingdom

66709127R00047